Published by Parragon in 2011

Parragon
Queen Street House
4 Queen Street
Bath BA1 1HE, UK

THE
LION KING

PaRragon

Bath • New York • Singapore • Hong Kong • Cologne • Delhi
Melbourne • Amsterdam • Johannesburg • Auckland • Shenzhen

'The Circle
of Life...'

The hot African sun rose on an amazing sight. Giraffes, zebras, elephants, and animals of all kinds were gathered at Pride Rock. This was an important day.

King Mufasa and Queen Sarabi watched as Rafiki, the wise baboon, presented their newborn son to the kingdom. The animals cheered and bowed to Prince Simba.

Simba grew into a playful and curious cub. Early one morning, Mufasa brought Simba to the top of Pride Rock.

'Everything the light touches is our kingdom,' he told his son. 'One day, the sun will set on my time here, and will rise with you as the new king.'

'Wow!' Simba cried. 'But what about that shadowy place?'

'You must never go across the border, Simba.' Mufasa said, sternly.

'But I thought a king can do whatever he wants!' said Simba.

Mufasa explained, 'There is more to being king than getting your way all the time. You need to respect all creatures. We are all connected in the great Circle of Life.'

Simba tried to listen, but he was too busy chasing caterpillars and practicing his pounce to pay attention to what his father was telling him.

Just then, Zazu arrived with news that hyenas had crossed into the Pride Lands!

Mufasa ordered Zazu to take Simba home, and ran off to battle the hyenas.

'I never get to go anywhere,' Simba complained.

Back at home, Simba went to see his uncle Scar.
'My dad just showed me the whole kingdom,' the cub
bragged. 'And I'm gonna rule it all!'

Scar was angry that he was no longer the next in
line to be king.

'Did he show you that place beyond the border?'
he asked Simba, slyly. 'Only the bravest of lions would
dare go to an elephant graveyard.'

Simba didn't see his uncle's evil trap. He decided
to show his father what a brave cub he could be.

'We're really going to
an elephant
graveyard!'

Simba set out to find his best friend, Nala. She was lying with their mothers on a rock nearby.

'Mom, can Nala and I go to this great place...near the water hole?' fibbed Simba.

'As long as Zazu goes with you,' answered Sarabi.

'We've got to ditch Zazu!' Simba whispered to Nala. 'We're really going to an elephant graveyard!'

Simba and Nala laughed as they ran in and out of animal herds to escape from Zazu. 'We've lost him!' cried Nala.

Together they played, laughing, tumbling, and rolling. Suddenly, with a thump, they landed next to a huge elephant skull!

They were in the Elephant Graveyard!

It was full of elephant skeletons, and the little cubs began to feel afraid.

Zazu caught up with them, but it was too late. Banzai, Shenzi, and Ed, three drooling hyenas, surrounded them!

The hyenas grabbed Zazu first. 'Why don't you pick on someone your own size?' shouted Simba, swiping his claws across the hyena's cheek.

'If you ever come near my son again...'

Suddenly, a tremendous roar shook the ground. It was Mufasa!

He fought off the hyenas bravely, whilst Zazu made sure that Simba and Nala escaped safely out of the way.

Mufasa's giant paw struck one of the hyenas, as he growled, 'If you ever come near my son again...'

The hyenas ran off before he had a chance to finish.

Mufasa scolded his son on the way home. 'You disobeyed me, Simba.'

'I was just trying to be brave, like you, Dad,' Simba said sadly.

'Being brave doesn't mean you go looking for trouble,' Mufasa replied.

Then Mufasa told Simba how the kings of the past looked down on them from the stars above.

'They will always be there to guide you Simba... and so will I.'

'I **will** be king!'

Scar was angry when the hyenas told him that
Simba had escaped. But he quickly came up with a new
plan to get rid of Simba and his father, and rallied an
army of hyenas.

'I will be king!' he cried.

The next day, Scar found Simba.

'Your father has a surprise for you,' Scar told
Simba, and led him down a steep gorge.

'Wait here,' he said to Simba.

Scar then signaled the hyenas to frighten a herd of wildebeest. The panicked animals stampeded right toward Simba!

Hearing the thunder of hooves, Mufasa looked into the gorge, and saw his son clinging to a branch. He leaped down, and saved Simba's life.

Simba was safe, but Mufasa was still in danger. As he tried to climb away from the stampede, the rocks crumbled beneath him.

Struggling up the cliff, Mufasa saw Scar looming above him.

'Brother, help me!' Mufasa cried.

Scar leaned forward and grabbed Mufasa's paws. But right at the last minute, he dug his sharp claws in!

'Long live the king!' Scar whispered, and flung Mufasa off the cliff. He disappeared into the herd below.

Simba had seen only that his father had fallen. He ran to his father and tried to wake him up, but Mufasa was dead.

Scar came to Simba's side. 'If it weren't for you,' he said, 'your father would still be alive! Run away, and never return!'

Heartbroken, Simba ran away as fast as he could. Scar sent the hyenas out to kill Simba, but the cub escaped them once more.

Scar announced to the Pride Lands the death of Mufasa and Simba, and that he would now be king.

Far away from the Pride Lands, the hot sun beat down on Simba. Exhausted, and unable to go any further, he slumped to the ground.

'We **saved** you!'

After a long while, Simba awoke. Everything around him looked different.

A meerkat named Timon and a warthog named Pumbaa had brought him to their home.

'We saved you!' cried Timon.

Pumbaa asked Simba where he was from, but Simba didn't want to answer. 'I did something terrible, but I don't want to talk about it.'

'You gotta put your worries behind you, kid!' said Timon. 'No worries...hakuna matata!'

Simba decided to stay with his new friends.

Years passed, and Simba grew into a young
lion. He had lots of fun with his friends, Timon
and Pumbaa.

One night, when they were looking up at the
stars, Simba remembered his father's words.

'Someone once told me that the great kings of
the past are up there, watching over us,' he said to
his friends.

The next day, Pumbaa was chasing a bug when a
fierce lioness sprang at him from the tall grass.

'She's gonna eat me!' Pumbaa squealed. Simba
heard his friend's cries and rushed to help.

'You're alive!'

Simba wrestled with the lioness, but soon realized it was his old friend, Nala!

'You're alive!' she said happily. 'That means you're the king!'

Nala told Simba how Scar had destroyed the Pride Lands, and how there was no food anymore.

'Simba, if you don't do something, everyone will starve.'

'I can't go back!' said Simba angrily, and he turned and walked away.

Later, Simba thought about what Nala had said.

'I won't go back,' he said to himself. 'It won't change anything.'

Just then, Simba heard a chanting song, coming from the jungle. Rafiki the baboon came walking toward him.

'If you want to see your father again, look down there,' Rafiki said, pointing into the pool of water next to them.

Simba saw the face of his father staring back at him.

'You see!' said Rafiki. 'He lives in you!'

Now Simba looked up and saw his father's face in the stars, 'Look inside yourself Simba. Remember who you are...you are my son, and the one true king.'

The next morning, Rafiki found Nala, Timon, and Pumbaa. He told them that Simba had returned to the Pride Lands.

'He's going to challenge his uncle!' Nala cried.

When Simba reached the Pride Lands, he was saddened by what he saw. His homeland that was once green and beautiful had turned barren under Scar's rule.

Bravely, Simba continued on his journey, to find his uncle.

When Simba arrived at Pride Rock, he let out a roar that shook the earth. Scar was surprised and frightened.

'This is my kingdom! Step down Scar!' shouted Simba. Scar ordered his hyenas to attack. They surrounded Simba and drove him to the edge of a cliff.

Simba grabbed onto the rocks as Scar stood above him.

'That's just how your father looked,' snarled Scar.

Then Simba realized it was Scar who had killed his father.

'This is my kingdom!

With new strength, Simba lunged onto the rock and attacked. Nala, Timon, and Pumbaa arrived, and a fight broke out on Pride Rock.

This time, Simba trapped Scar at the steep edge of Pride Rock. Sparing his life, he ordered his uncle to run away and never return.

Scar pretended to leave, but then turned and lunged at Simba. Simba swiped his great claw, and Scar fell to his death in the gorge below.

Simba took his rightful place as the Lion King, and once again the Pride Lands flourished.

Soon, all the animals gathered at Pride Rock, including Zazu, Timon, and Pumbaa, to celebrate the birth of Simba and Nala's cub. A new celebration of life took place, with Rafiki holding the cub up for all the kingdom to see.

The Circle of Life would continue.